My Ratchet Secret

Disclaimer:

This is a work of fiction. Names, characters, businesses, places, events and incidents are either the products of the author's imagination or used in a fictitious manner. Any resemblance to actual persons, living or dead, or actual events is purely coincidental.

D1367913

Hard Letting Go

"Damn I miss my baby sis" Adrian agonized as he laid fresh roses and carnations on his sister Tasha's grave. "I swear I would give up a limb to have her back again," he cried.

"Come on bae; let's head back to the car."

I placed a comforting hand on his shoulder as I tried to coax him away from the grave site.

"The shit just makes me mad as hell!" he sobbed. "I live for the day they catch the son of a bitch who did this to her."

Adrian's grief turned to anger each time he thought about his sister being robbed and stabbed to death in her own driveway. Even though there was nothing he could do he still blamed himself for not being there for her.

From the time his baby sister was born his grandfather had instilled in him the importance of taking care of family. He told him "no matter what, always protect your sister and your momma." Those were paw paw's words that he tried his damndest to live by.

His grandfather was a proud man with old southern values. He believed in taking care of home first. He was old school in the mentality that women were the weaker sex and needed someone to watch out for them. For that very reason he wouldn't hesitate to bust a cap at any nigga that thought about screwing over any of his sister's. And he carried these same teaching down to his own sons and grandsons.

Adrian enlisted in the Army when he was fresh out of high school. His visit home on his 28th birthday would be the last time he would see his sister alive.

"I should have listened to paw paw, I should have protected her."

"Bae how long are you going to keep blaming yourself? What could you have possibly done differently if you were there?"

"I could have helped her out more financially so she wouldn't have to depend on them sorry muthafuckas she use to deal with. Maybe she could have moved out the ghetto to a safer neighborhood.... every time you look up somebody was getting killed over there."

It was true; she lived in one of the most dangerous neighborhoods on the west side. Stabbings and shooting were norm and pretty much went unsolved due to the city's high crime rate.

I wanted to tell my fiancé that a person could be a target anywhere but I knew it would fall on deaf ears. It was useless, he was hell bent on blaming himself. My only mission was to get him home and to try and cheer him up.

My plan was to grab something quick to eat on the way home and spend the rest of the day deciding on who I wanted to be my bride's maids in my wedding. I had finally landed the man of my dreams and I wanted my wedding day to be perfect. That would all have to be put on hold at least for tonight. My man needed some special attention and I knew just the thing to make him feel better.

Cater To You

"Damn bae I told you all this wasn't necessary. I'm cool." Adrian took a deep breath and eased down into the hot bath I had drawn for him. He leaned back and let out a sigh of relief as the jets pulsated away the tension of the day.

"It wasn't necessary but you haven't passed up anything up so far" I giggled playfully. That included the steak and king crab I threw down on for dinner. Now it was time for desert, freaky style.

"Hush girl, come on in here and join me."

"Not yet daddy," with that I winked and sashayed out of the room.

I returned with a double shot of Remy, a fat blunt and a stack of ones. "This should hold you over till I get back," I cooed.

Adrian reveled in the fact that this meant I was going to shake that ass for him. The portable stripper pole was still up from a few weeks ago, but he had no idea he was going to get treated again so soon.

Once I was back in our master suite I took a toke off of my own weed pipe before slipping into a crotchless fishnet cat suit and red thigh high patent leather boots. My girl Soon Lee had hooked me up with the baddest

China doll lace front that money could buy. It was silky straight and jet black with Chinese bangs and it swung at an impressive 26 inches. Nothing was too good for my boo. I had been paying on this wig for three months and finally got her out the layaway.

Before long I queued up the music.

"Make it rain trick."

"Make it make it rain trick."

"Aww shit!" Adrian howled as I twerked my way in the room before dropping it low.   "These hoes don't have shit on my baby!"

With that he stood up revealing his stiff 10 inches of manhood as he made it rain while I clapped my ass and made it bounce with a precision that would have made any stripper jealous.

No matter how many times he saw me naked he was always smitten. I was truly one of the most beautiful women he had ever seen; at least that's what he told me. I stood at an even 5'8 inches and had curves for days. He told me that I had the most voluptuous ass he had ever seen on such a slim frame. Most women had to slave at the gym for what came natural to me. I had full sexy lips and a pair of bedroom eyes that would make any brotha stop in his tracks. And my cocoa brown skin was as supple as a baby's ass. That was one of the things that he says he loves about his baby was the fact of how meticulous I am with my skincare regimen.

Shit as far as he was concerned I was the best of the best. He had never had a woman to cater to him the way I did. All his friends were envious at the fact that I would get up every morning an hour before he did to make sure I looked my best. By the time he was done getting ready for work I would have his breakfast made before getting myself ready for work.

My head game was on point and we won't even go there on the good good. He would be a damn fool not to wife this.

It had gotten to the point where he couldn't take it any longer. He was hard as a rock and ready to tap this ass.

"Damn you sexy as fuck, imma tear that ass up" he bellowed as emerged from the tub and walked towards me. The steam arose from his glistening biceps.

He raked his belongings to the side on the dresser, picked me up and sat me in front of him. He dropped to knees and began fondling my full C cups before finally releasing them and teasing my nipples through the net. I arched my back as he slid his tongue in my mouth before moving over to my neck. I was sopping wet at this point. My pussy throbbed as he worked his way down with his full lips sucking on my erect nipples. He tore at the opening in my body stocking to make it large enough for him to enter and to finger my wetness.

"Ohh bae that feels so good," I moaned.

Adrian was so aroused from my performance there wasn't going to be any playing around tonight. It was time to get down to business. After we stood He slammed me against the wall, lifted my leg and plunged his thick dick deep inside of me.

"Oh shit! It feels sooo good" I whimpered. I had been waiting for this dick all day and this nigga was putting it down!

Before I knew it he had spun me around and bent me over. His hands roamed freely over my smooth round ass, gripping and spanking as he drove his dick deep between my legs. I let out a moan as his thick manhood sunk inch by inch into my starving hot slit.

I bounced my ass against him to meet his thrusts. The more I groaned the more he fucked me hard and mercilessly causing my tits to bounce uncontrollably. The walls of my pussy were stretched to their limit as Adrian's dick grew with each stroke. Pretty soon I was stuck by wave after wave of ecstasy as my pussy pulsated from a massive orgasm.

"Your pussy is so fucking tight and good" Adrian grunted as he lost control as began to thrust me deeply.

"Fuck me hard daddy" I whimpered. He started pumping me at lightning speed, eventually letting out a howl as he exploded inside of me. My snatch was like a vice grip milking every drop of cum he expelled.

Once we had finished I lay across Adrian's lap and basked in the moment.

"Damn bae you sure know how to take my mind off of shit that's bothering me."

"It was no big deal you know I don't mind taking care of you," I responded while lightly stroking his thigh.

"And that's the very reason I'm gonna try my best to make you the happiest woman in the world once we get married," he replied.

"You already do that now, the ring will just make it official. I have so much planning to do. I need to be working on the invitations as we speak."

"Speaking of that; baby when are you going to talk to your family? You keep promising me that I'm going to get to meet them but you keep putting it off."

This was the only thing that gave Adrian cold feet about marrying me. He had yet to meet my family. If it were any one of his friends he would tell them that this was a huge red flag and to proceed with caution, however when it came to his own situation he failed to practice what he preached.

However, in his mind it wasn't without good reason. I measured up to everything he was looking for in a woman. I was funny, smart, beautiful, educated and sensitive all rolled into one sexy package. I never hesitated to take care of his needs inside the bedroom and out. He knew my parents were deceased as well as my maternal grandmother who raised me. And so that only left my cousins and a few aunts and uncles that I wasn't really close with.

Regardless of this fact Adrian still wanted to meet the family that I did have and invite them to the wedding. He had come from a close knit family so he told me couldn't imagine what it must be like losing my parents so young.

"I keep putting it off because as I've said on many occasions I really don't deal with them like that. The few aunts that I was close to I haven't spoken to in years. We just kinda grew apart," I responded hoping Adrian would change the subject.

"Bae, promise me you will call them tomorrow."

"I tell you what, I have the day off so I will make it my point to try and catch up with someone. Maybe one of my cousins has some contact numbers."

Adrian leaned down and kissed me on the forehead. "Thanks baby, you won't be sorry. Just wait and see. They will probably be glad to hear from you."

I nodded my head reassuringly. "You're probably right."

Family Ties

After preparing Adrian's breakfast and seeing him off to work I poured myself a shot of cognac and began to pace the floor. The conversation from the night before had me beyond vexed. I began slamming pots and pans around the kitchen and yelling to myself.

"Niggas ain't ever fucking satisfied! I done already told his ass that I don't keep contact with my family but he just got to keep pressing the damn issue!"

"I don't understand what the big fucking deal is!" I raged as I kicked over the kitchen trash can, causing debris to fly everywhere. After which I stormed around the house snatching up clothes and cramming them into the hamper.

"I cook, I clean, I fuck him when he wants to be fucked, and I comfort him when he's grieving. What the hell else does he want from me? I done spent $1,500 on that damn lace front, bought all them damn stripper clothes, and for what? I know there ain't a bitch out here that can twerk it like me but his ass wanna keep whining about meeting a damn family!"

I finished downing my drink and was about to continue my rant when the phone rang. When I picked it up and looked at the caller ID I saw that it was Adrian and my demeanor totally changed.

"Hello"

"Hey bae did I leave my driver's license there?"

"I don't know sweetie, lemme check," I responded softly. "Where do you think you might have left it?"

"It's usually in my wallet but I took it out. I think it's in the pants I wore yesterday," he responded.

"I just gathered up the laundry, hang on a second. Nope it's not in here. I'll check your dresser."

"Damn I thought it was in there. I'm on my way back home anyway. I was hoping I would find it and save myself a trip."

Panic immediately set in when I heard Adrian was returning. I was up in the bedroom but I needed to make my way downstairs and make sure he didn't see the mess I had just made. Plus I needed to swish with some mouth wash really quick. It was 8am and I didn't drink alcohol that early, at least as far as he knew.

"Ok I'll keep looking," I panted as I raced downstairs and quickly began to pick up the trash that was strewn about the kitchen.

"You sound like you out of breath, what the hell you doing?" he asked.

"I'm running around the house looking for YOUR license. I just ran down the stairs." I had to hurry up and think of a lie to cover for why I sounded so winded on the phone.

"Well damn if you sounding like that you need to hit the gym," Adrian chuckled.

"Shut the hell up."

"Hey baby never mind I found it in the glove compartment. I'm headed back to work. Talk to you later."

I had never been so relieved in my entire life. This called for another shot.

Once I sat down and caught my breath I picked up the phone, pushed *67 so my number would be blocked from the caller ID on the other end and dialed.

"Hello"

"Hey momma"

"Hey sweetie, how are you?"

"I'm good momma, I saw you that called my cell the other day and I just wanted to return your call. I know that you had your church board meeting yesterday so I didn't want to bother you."

"Well it's good to hear from you. What number are you dialing from? I almost didn't answer. You I know I don't pick up for unknown numbers" momma laughed. "I had a feeling that it might be you."

"Huh? Oh… I'm calling from my cell, it does that sometimes. Anyway what have you been up to?"

"Nothing child, this old arthritis keeps acting up but you know I ain't letting nothing keep me down. Lord willing I'm going to the church picnic this weekend."

"That sounds like fun, how's daddy?"

"He's ok, just as old and crazy as ever. I thought you was gonna try and get down this way."

This way was actually Memphis Tennessee; my parents had moved there from DC after all the kids left home. My parents hadn't seen me in over three years since I myself had relocated before they made their move. It was hell trying to convince momma and daddy that I was ok over the phone. And that I was constantly working overtime and couldn't get time off. Momma asked me to visit each time we spoke, daddy had pretty much given up. It hurt me that they couldn't be a part of my special day. As a matter of fact my parents had no idea that I had moved back to DC, had met someone, and was engaged.

"On everything I love I will be there this summer, I swear."

"Hush up with all that swearing," momma scolded. "You been going to church and reading your bible? I just worry about you so much. It's been so long since we have seen you. I know you can't be that busy."

I laughed to try and ease the awkwardness from lying to my momma but I could never really hide anything from her. "I haven't been doing either as much as I should momma, but imma do better. And you know I love you and daddy; I've just been so tied up working all these doubles, but I'm making it my business this year to get down there to you guys no matter what."

Momma was a trooper. She knew I was lying through my teeth but she was way beyond begging me to visit over and over, after she said her piece that was it. I guess she was tired of beating a dead horse. And at the end of the day as long as she could hear my voice and knew in her heart that I was ok she was good. She didn't pressure me because she knew that I would come around in my own time.

"Well alright, I didn't want anything when I called. I won't hold you up. I just wanted to talk to my baby."

"Ok momma I love you. Tell daddy I said hello and I love him."

"Love you too baby."

For Better Or For Worse

By the time Adrian had gotten home from work everything was back on track. The house was spotless, dinner was cooked and I made sure I had myself put together as well. The stress from my morning was nothing but a faint memory at this point. I hoped that by today Adrian would have forgotten all about the calls I was supposed to make to my family.

"That shit needs to be water under the bridge," I said to myself. Hopefully he will be too tired to go there. His usual routine after work was to eat dinner and chat it up with me for a bit before either popping in a movie or vegging out with his Call of Duty video game. I really hoped that would be that case tonight so I could get some much needed work done for the wedding.

I needed to get the invitation list done and set up an appointment for cake tasting. Those things were on my short to do list that was about a mile long. Adrian had already told me that I didn't have to feel like I was doing everything by myself. He offered to help every step of the way, which was something very rare with all the guys I had ever met. That's one of the things that made him so special, was the fact that I never felt like I was "in it" alone. He made me feel like he was there for me no matter what. He even offered to hire a wedding planner but I insisted on taking care of the details myself. Even though I figured I would be a basket case by the time I walked down the aisle I was beyond thrilled that I was marrying the man that I had fell in love with the first time I laid eyes on him.

"Something smells good up in here, what you cooking bae" Adrian greeted me with kiss and kicked his shoes off.

"Meatloaf, mac and cheese, collard greens, and banana pudding for desert."

"Damn that sounds good, I'm starving. They worked the shit outta my ass today. Shit I should have come back home, and stayed."

While we were eating dinner I listened to Adrian's vent session about his bosses and crazy ass coworkers before asking me about my day.

"So what have you been up too all day?" he asked as he spooned himself up a heaping serving of banana pudding.

I laughed "Do you really have to ask? I finally got an appointment with that bakery everybody has been raving about. And I think I have narrowed down my choices of bridesmaid dresses to three."

"Did you make that phone call?" he asked looking at me with a raised eyebrow.

"*Here we fucking go again!*" I thought. "Nah... I didn't get a chance."

Adrian was immediately pissed.

"So you didn't even try and call your cousin? I thought we agreed on that last night Pebbles," he grumbled.

"Bae I have been busy all day long, I had to run errands, do laundry, clean up, and the dinner didn't just cook itself you know?" I was fuming inside but I tried my best not to show it.

He sat stone faced as he listened to my excuse.

"You know what? You are full of excuses. Every time we get on the subject of your family it's gotta be a big damn deal. How would you feel if you never met any of my people Pebbles? Shit I was damn near ready to show you off the day I met you. But naw a brotha like me ain't even good enough to meet the little family you do have."

With that he got up from the table and headed for the den with me close on his heels.

"Baby let me explain...I."

Before I could finish he cut me off. "Just drop it!"

Adrian didn't make a point of raising his voice at me but his anger had now turned to resentment. I was perfect in every other way but this was the one thing that was hanging over our heads causing drama in our relationship. Adrian was hurt and angry. He was crazy about me and would do anything in the world for me but this was one area when he put his foot down and he wasn't budging.

He told me that sometimes he would ask himself why it was so important to meet my family since I said I didn't really deal with them. Why couldn't he just accept that and move on?

Part of the reason was despite the fact that he loved and trusted me he said that his gut told him that I was hiding something in that area. No matter how much he tried to shake the feeling he always felt like something wasn't quite right with that whole situation.

Another reason was he didn't want any surprises AFTER we got married. He didn't have any intentions on backing out of the wedding but the way I seemed so hell bent on keeping everything about them a secret was starting to make him second guess his decision. Hell we might have to put everything on hold till we get to the bottom of this.

I could see that Adrian was hurt and disappointed. He had never raised his voice at me in the whole two years we were together. It was obvious that I couldn't keep feeding him the same lies about not having time to contact anyone. Not only was he stubborn and not bending in this situation it seemed like he was beginning to get more suspicious as the days passed. There was no way that I was about to lose my fiancé over this bullshit right here. This called for drastic measures.

After letting Adrian cool down for about an hour I went back in the den.

"Baby we need to talk," I agonized.

Adrian looked at me with knitted brows and maintained his cold disposition.

"About what?" he grunted.

"About us"

I could tell that he wanted very much to carry out his grudge for the rest of the evening and possibly the next day also but upon closer inspection he could tell that I was choked up and it piqued his attention.

"What's on your mind?" he asked softening his tone.

"I wanna talk about my family….. I don't know how to tell you this so I'm just gonna come right out and say it. My parents aren't really dead."

Adrian's mouth fell open. He paused his game, sat up straight and looked at me.

"You damn sure got my attention. What you mean your parents ain't dead?"

"Well at least not to my knowledge." The tears began to etch their way down my cheeks as I shared my story.

"My daddy left us when we was little. I was the oldest so I remember the most. He use to beat the shit outta my momma. They both was on crack so when he wasn't going upside her head or getting high he had her working the strip."

I blew my nose before continuing. "My momma sold her body for crack while they was together and after he left us I guess the pressure got to be too much and she walked out on us too." I looked down at the wet tissue in my hands to avoid making eye contact.

Adrian got up and came over to the love seat where I was sitting and put his arm around me.

"Damn bae, why you lie to me? You know you can tell me anything?"

"I was ashamed. You was raised by both of your parents and you are close to everybody in your family. Plus everybody is doing well, they all successful.

"I can dig that but you shouldn't be ashamed of where you come from."

"That's easy for you to say, everybody didn't grow up in the Huxtable household like you did. Many nights I went to bed hungry cause I gave the little bit of food I could steal to my little brother and sister. You just don't know what I've been through. Your family seemed so perfect I didn't want to share all that ratchet bullshit I been through. I thought you wouldn't want me anymore.

Luckily I was old enough to fend for myself but child protective services wanted to pick me up and put me in a foster home like they did my lil sis and brother. The only reason they didn't get me was cause I ran every time I saw them. I spent half of my damn childhood running. And I'm still running… running from my past.

When I met you I had never had anybody treat me as good as you have. I ain't never loved nobody the way I love you. I never meant to hurt you by lying to you, but I found love and somebody who loved me back and I was too scared of losing it, losing you…" With that I broke down, trembling and sobbing uncontrollably.

Adrian held me tight and wiped my tears away. Hearing how much I had endured from my childhood touched him to the point he found his own eyes welling up. It tore him up to see me this way.

"Damn baby I'm so sorry" he whispered through his own veil of tears.

"Now you see why I wanted to just leave the past in the past? It's just too painful for me to deal with Adrian. I didn't want this shit to ever come out but you just had to keep pressing the issue. Now I'm all fucked up. I had that shit buried deep inside."

He would later tell me that it was at that very moment he realized maybe he had been pressing too hard for something that shouldn't have really matter. If I hadn't seen my family in years who was he to keep pressuring me to meet people my ass barely even knew? From that day forward he said he would let that shit die. He had a down ass woman on his team and the past didn't matter as long as I treated him good.

"I'm glad you told me the truth. I'm sorry I was pressing so you hard. I guess I should have just trusted that you weren't hiding anything that was gonna hurt me."

I looked him in his eyes with a stare of intent. "I would NEVER do anything to hurt you. I love you too damn much."

"I love you too bae."

"Now can we PLEASE put this shit behind us and never bring it up again?" I asked.

"Damn right we can put it behind us, but you gotta admit it must feel like a weight done been lifted from off your shoulders."

Secrets And Lies

One year later

This was it, the day I had finally been dreaming of, my wedding day. I had been planning for this day for over a year and with that being said there was no detail left unturned. My only regret? My parents, siblings and my best friend couldn't be here to celebrate my happiness.

I grew up in Washington DC with one of the best families a person could ask for. My mother was a God fearing, church going woman. She was not only momma to me and my younger sister and brother she was known as momma around the community as well. She didn't hesitate to help anyone that was in need. Momma would give a stranger the shoes off of her feet rather than see them go barefoot. I only hope I can become half the woman she is someday.

My father was a master electrician by trade although he dabbled in plumbing and dry walling as well. He has owned his own business for over thirty years and pretty much taught me the value of owning your own and having your own. His motto was always: "Why give somebody else a day's work that you could be giving yourself?" Damn I miss daddy, hopefully we can see each other again someday.

My younger sister Bria grew up to be one of the baddest hair dressers DC had ever seen. She kept everybody's shit in the neighborhood laid. Last I heard she had taken her skills to Atlanta where she was supposed to be opening her own shop.

My brother Meeko (Meek to family and friends) is an aspiring rapper. He could usually be found either sitting around making beats or writing lyrics. As you can just about guess my parents wasn't having that shit. Rapping was all fine and dandy but they insisted that he get his education as well. He was in his fourth year of college studying to be an engineer while taking the campus by storm in every rap battle that came up as well as hosting his own college radio show on the weekends.

Yeah, I guess you could say my parents did a damn good job when it came to raising us. Although it seems like they dropped the ball with me. Maybe they were young and inexperienced as parents. Or maybe they just didn't know how to deal with the fact that their oldest son was gay.

Yes that's my ratchet secret I'm really a man, well that's part of it. I wasn't always Pebbles. I was born as Peyton Edward Jones. I have always known that I was different than the rest of the boys in my hood. I didn't like the same things they liked, and that included girls. As a matter of fact the time they spent playing sports and chasing girls I spent perfecting my makeup game and admiring women's fashions.

Unlike many gay kids I didn't have to "come out" to my parents. They already suspected that something was *off* with me from a very young age.

I loved playing dress up in my mother's clothes as well as wearing her shoes around the house. When they sat me down to have the "talk" I flat out told them that I didn't like girls and to take it a step further I felt like a girl myself, in every way imaginable. I was transgender as well.

I have always envied my beautiful girlfriends and would do anything in my power to look like them. Simply put I felt like I was born in the wrong body. I struggled for many years to suppress the jealousy and anger that I felt for my younger sister because she was born as a girl. "Why couldn't it have been me?" is what I would ask myself as I would cry myself to sleep many nights.

Despite the fact that I was gay and transgender my parents still loved me and although they were Christians and they didn't accept my lifestyle, they never made me feel bad for my choices. I was one of the lucky ones. Besides the lectures momma and daddy gave on how being gay was a sin and that I could "pray it away" I never had to endure the hurt and backlash that many homosexuals did with their own families. Even when momma's church going friends tried to label me as a demon she always stuck up for me and loved me regardless. My torment would come later down the line when I pushed society's norms of dressing in drag and identifying myself as a woman.

Tasha Ramsey was my very best friend in the whole world. If there was anyone that I loved almost as much as my boo Adrian it was Tasha. She never ridiculed me or judged me. She loved me for who I was. She was another driving force in helping to mold me into the person I am today. Like I said I was damn lucky to have the people closest to me in my corner. It made all the difference in the world. Tasha was that friend that you had growing up that you not only had fun with but got in trouble with as well. We were thick as thieves and there was no separating us. I have so much love for her that I can't help but shed a tear every time she comes to mind.

When I met her brother Adrian I was sprung. Even as a kid he was as cute as he could be. I had been crushing on him from day one but when he grew up it was a wrap. He grew from a skinny little kid that liked playing kickball and chasing the ice cream truck down the road into a fine sexy ass man. He stood at an impressive six feet three inches, had smooth Mahogany skin and a face that sported features so chiseled it should have been in a museum.

He wasn't a player but he damn sure had his share of girlfriends. I would have done anything back then to be in their shoes. The problem was he was as straight as the day was long. And to make matters worse not only did he barely know I existed. He made it a point to steer clear of me at all costs. He wanted nothing to do with his sister's "gay ass friend." This hurt me to the core. Talk about unrequited love! I would have done anything to be with Adrian but he wouldn't even give me the time of day even as a friend. By the time we were all young adults he was able to "tolerate" me but still fed me from a long handled spoon.

I stood back for over a year and watched his present girlfriend treat him like shit while he damn near worshipped the ground she walked on. She didn't deserve him. She didn't deserve to get the love and affection that I should have been getting. I was determined to make Adrian mine no matter what the cost.

This would ultimately help me seal the decision to have sex reassignment surgery. If he didn't want me as a man I would have no choice but to become a woman. The choice wasn't hard seeing as I already considered myself to be a woman any way. And when it was all said and done I planned on being the baddest bitch that he ever laid eyes on.

I had to figure out some way to get my hands on that type of money. There was no way momma and daddy was going to loan it to me. I had already expressed to them how much it would mean to me if I could have the surgery seeing as I wasn't comfortable in my own skin. Their response was just what was to be expected. I was born a man child so I should accept the fact that I was in a man's body and that God don't make no mistakes. My girl Tasha was in my corner but she was just as broke as me. We had just graduated high school and didn't have a pot to piss in. Part time gigs at the mall and local fast food restaurants just weren't cutting it. I needed big money and I needed it fast.

Where was an average poor kid in the hood going to come up with over $300,000? Plus before I could even think about surgery I had to have to endure a considerable amount of counseling and psychiatric assessments. After the surgery there would be prescription charges, speech therapy, and hair removal from face and body just to name a few of the many expenses. I would also need hormone replacement therapy and a whole new wardrobe on top of the surgery. Lucky Adrian had enlisted in the Army after his senior year. This would give me a chance to come up with a plan of action.

Going against my girl Tasha's pleas, who was now away at college, I decided that I would strip for the money. There were several gay clubs around town that hopped on the weekends and I just needed to find my niche. I was determined not to let a bitch out do me, man or woman.

I got my shit together and ditched those tired ass wigs I was wearing for only top of the line hair. I made sure I was waxed from head to toe, body was tight and my face was beat every night. There was no way these hoes were going to outshine me. I was getting my money even if it meant turning a few tricks with the so called straight men that snuck in to see me perform. It didn't take long for momma to realize where I was stepping out to every night and she demanded that I stopped or get out on my own.

That's when I decided to get my own apartment so I could have the privacy I needed. Before I knew it I was not only dancing but tricking as well, full time. The money I needed came with ease seeing as I was making upwards to $2,000 a night. I did this for several years till I racked up the cash I needed as well as a nice nest egg.

From doing my research I decided that it was going to be cheaper to have most of my procedures done out of the country. Plus I didn't want just any old Dr. I wanted the best plastic surgeon my money could buy. I needed to look as close to a natural woman as possible to fool Adrian and for my own satisfaction. That included my soon to be lady parts as well.

I decided that I was going to Korea. I spoke of this to no one. As far as my parents and Tasha was concerned I had moved to another state, and was working a ton of overtime. This was the excuse as to why they couldn't visit me. In reality they thought I was still "in the streets," little did they know I had other plans. I played right into whatever role they wanted me too when we spoke but never once disclosed my secret.

Dr Rim Yoon would not only become my sex reassignment surgeon, he would be my primary care physician for the two years I spent recovering and learning all the ins and outs of what was needed to maintain the surgery and to convince everyone who saw me that I was a woman and not a man "playing dress up."

When I finally moved back to my home town I had a totally new outlook on life. I was a woman! I got myself an apartment and a more respectful job as fashion consultant at a prestige modeling agency. My stripping and hoeing days were over! I had yet to let my family or Tasha know I was back in town. My parents had since moved on to Tennessee. I wasn't ready to reveal my secret just yet. I needed to see how it would play out first. Plus I had a few things that I needed to master, from my mannerisms down to my walk. I wanted to be perfect.

Niggas were already starting to hit on me as a woman and I couldn't have been more thrilled. Dr Yoon had gone over and above the call of duty. All I needed to do now was find out when my boo was on another leave. That wouldn't be hard because all I needed to do was call Tasha. My biggest challenge was dealing with the change in my voice since my trachea shave. That didn't matter I would just tell her I was coming down with something. Once I found out when Adrian was coming home I planned my next move.

Tasha said that he would be staying at their parents' home so I made it a point to survey the house day and night to track his moves. When we ran into each other in the grocery store it wasn't by accident. I made sure that I was fine as hell, smelling good, toes done, the works.

After following him inside the store I conveniently spilled the fruit that I had bagged up when he walked by the produce section. I made sure my saline babies were greased up and sitting right up in his face when he bent down to help me. That nigga didn't know what hit him! He was all up on my ass and I loved every minute of it! I FINALLY had Adrian lusting after ME for a change.

Another crusty muthafucka tried to roll up and start making eye contact and shit while we were exchanging numbers. He just don't know, I would have caught a case that day if he would have cock blocked my shit!

We would run into each other several more times before he finally got up the nerve to ask me out. Little did he know that shit wasn't a coincidence, I had planned my moves like a game of chess and I wasn't about to lose. I wasn't stopping till I made him mine. Oh yes Adrian Ramsey would be my husband.

Between Lovers And Friends

My plan was a success. In the three months that Adrian spent at home we had become an item. He had fallen for me pretty quickly. And as you would guess there was no need for me to fall for him. I had been in love with him since we were children. I was literally living my dream. I was now a beautiful sexy woman, I had a good job and I had landed my man.

My luck would finally run out when Adrian invited his sister Tasha over to visit without my knowledge. He had been begging me to meet his family but I kept putting it off for fear I would be recognized. Aside from talking to Tasha on the phone we hadn't seen each other in years and she had no idea that I was back in town or that I was now a woman. I guess he got tired of waiting and decided to invite Tasha over for dinner at my place the night before he was due to go back to active duty. Luckily his parents were out of town for a funeral or they would have been there also.

Whoever said that you can't hide shit from a good friend was exactly right. Tasha recognized me as soon as we met. I remember it like it was yesterday.

"Tasha I want you to meet my baby Pebbles, Pebbles meet my sister Tasha," announced Adrian as he introduced us.

"Please to meet you Tasha."

"Nice to meet you too" she responded looking me over from head to toe.

"He's told me so much about you," I responded nervously.

I tried to keep the conversation light hoping this heffa wouldn't start running off at the mouth.

"Uhmm… yeah, same here."

"You alright sis? Look like you done seen a damn ghost" asked Adrian.

"Oh naw... Pebbles just looks like somebody I know, kinda caught me off guard," she replied, glaring at me suspiciously.

The whole time I was thinking to myself, *"this hoe betta not even think about blowing my cover."*

We ended up having a nice dinner that evening and Tasha never spoke a word to Adrian about her suspicion. Who knows maybe she didn't recognize me after all. Or just maybe she was the best friend that I remembered, who realized who I was, but was happy for me and my new life. In any case the night ended on a pleasant note with Adrian none the wiser. After my baby left the next morning I got a surprise visit from Tasha.

"We need to talk," she announced boldly.

"Well good morning to you too" I responded sarcastically.

"I just wanted to come back and look at you again. Just what the hell do you think you're doing?"

"Excuse me? You just met me yesterday so I can't even imagine what kinda of drama you think you are about to roll up in here and start."

Tasha stormed past me and stood in the living room.

"Cut the shit Peyton, I know who you are. What kind of fucked up game are you trying to pull on my brother?"

"Peyton? Who the hell is Peyton?" I asked trying to get my bluff in.

"Did you hear what I said? I know it's you! The only reason I didn't bust your ass out yesterday at dinner was because my brother is all in love and shit and I didn't want to burst his bubble," Tasha fumed while circling me, looking me up and down. "Damn you really did it. Is that where you've been all this time?"

That was it, the gig was up. She had found me out. I didn't think that I would be seeing my best friend again under these circumstances but life has a funny sense of humor.

"I did what I had to do and I don't have any regrets. I can't believe how you just gon' run up in here flapping off at the mouth and not even ask how I'm doing. So do you like what you see?"

I was too out done. This was supposed to be my girl and all she was worried about is how I looked. You would think since she hadn't seen me in years she would be glad that I'm doing good.

"Ask how you doing? You had me and your parents worried sick about yo' ass. You know how many nights yo' momma called me crying and shit 'cause yo' behind was deep in them streets and wasn't trying to hear shit we had to say? Then you just upped and left. How the hell you think that made me feel? That shit hurt Peyton so don't run yo' damn pity party on me. And when yo' ass do return you a damn woman, and done hooked up with my brother? This shit is unreal!"

"The name is Pebbles, and I ain't asking for nobody's fucking pity."

At this point I was beyond upset. My damn heart was racing and I was griming her ass like she stole my favorite pair of shoes. The nerve of this hoe!

"Pebbles my ass! I'm calling you Peyton! All that shit you done had done to yourself don't make you a woman."

If it were anyone else I would have slapped the taste out of their mouth behind that remark, but Tasha's words cut me deep. I wanted so badly for my friend to be happy for me. I can't believe she went there after all we had been through. She was one of the few people in the world that knew how conflicted I was with the body I was in. I think the reason it hurt me so bad was because this was the first real reaction from someone who really knew my true identity. Someone who I thought loved me.

My hands started to tremble and my throat tightened up. Before I knew it I had broken down in tears. I hated being this vulnerable but sometimes when your past comes back to stare you in the face it don't always come bearing good news. It comes to drudge up painful memories. Memories of not being accepted by the man I loved with all my heart and soul. I finally had him now and I wasn't looking back. And if it meant that my best friend would now be the one that turned on me, so be it. I was determined to have myself a happily ever after with Adrian.

As I stood with my back towards her the tears flowed freely. She ended her rant, walked over to me and touched me on the shoulder.

"I'm sorry Peyton... I mean Pebbles. I didn't mean that."

"It's all good; you said what was on your mind."

"I said what I said out of anger, shock and surprise. This shit is crazy for me. The last time I saw you, you were a man. Well at least you were in a man's body, but that's still no excuse for what I said."

With that we embraced and cried like a mother and child being reunited.

"I accept your apology, I missed y'all so much. I didn't plan on going away like I did but I was on a mission."

When we finally let go of one another Tasha spun me around.

"For the record you do look beautiful."

"Thank you boo."

I wish I could have frozen that moment in time. For those few moments we were like teenagers again. I loved Tasha and I know she loved me but that wasn't enough to stop the pink elephant in the room from being addressed. The bonding moment was short lived. Tasha would soon revert back to the original reason she stopped by; to talk about Adrian.

"I love you and I missed you but this is some foul shit right here. When do you plan on telling my brother who you really are? I know he's gonna lose it when he finds out."

I stood there silently rolling my eyes and twirling a lock of hair. I had no intentions of telling Adrian shit.

"Wait, so you were never gonna tell him? That's fucked up! My brother is not gay. He needs to be told the truth so HE can make the decision whether or not he can live with it."

"Look Tasha it's like this. I'm not telling Adrian a damn thing. You know how he felt about me when he knew I was a man. I'm not gonna sit up here and try to pretend that I'm not wrong for what I'm doing but I love him. I have always loved him. You know how the song goes: if loving Adrian is wrong I don't wanna be right. I know you mad but I would never do anything to hurt your brother."

"Never do anything to hurt him? You're living a lie Peyton! Wake up! So what if he didn't want you as a man, hello, he's straight. Move on, I can't believe you went this far. I don't even know who you are anymore, for real. Do your parents know?"

"I planned on telling them when the time is right."

At this point tempers were flared. Tasha was livid that I had betrayed her brother and I was beside myself at the fact that she couldn't just leave well enough alone and be happy for me. It wasn't like I was hurting anyone. Adrian was happy and none the wiser. I wasn't about to let her fuck our shit up. I tried once again to talk some sense into her.

"I'm not letting you go through with this bullshit. That's my brother we are talking about," she announced.

"And I'm your best friend. Are you saying that blood is thicker than water?" I asked trying to make a grab for her hand before she snatched away.

"Correction, you *were* my best friend. A friend wouldn't even think about doing the shit that you are trying to pull. And the fact that you think it's nothing wrong with it is really twisted. You done completely lost yo' damn mind. If you don't think I will tell my brother you got me all fucked up!"

With that she headed for the front door.

I begged and pleaded with her not to tell him. I even blocked the door in an effort to talk her down before she did something stupid.

"Please I'm begging you! Don't tell Adrian. I'll tell him I promise."

"You really must think I'm boo boo the fool. You had plenty of time to tell him. Your ass was planning on not saying shit but your cover was blown. Now move out the damn way," she scowled as she pushed me aside.

I couldn't deny the fact that she was telling the truth about everything but despite the facts that were laid out on the table I couldn't let her tell Adrian the truth.

"Please let me tell him myself Tasha. He's already going to be crushed. I got myself into this mess. At least let me be the one to tell him the truth. I will come clean with him, I give you my word."

I wasn't saying shit to Adrian but I had to slow this bitch down She was about to put a monkey wrench in my whole plan.

"You got 24 hours."

"Tasha you know that he doesn't have a phone with him. I have to wait for him to call me. I need more time.

"You have one week. When he calls you, you better tell him the truth if you don't I will" she snapped before walking out the door and letting it slam behind her.

End Of The Road

As I sat in the tub for over an hour reflecting on all the events that had transpired in my life I realized that I was now faced with the difficult decision of choosing between my best friend and the man I loved. There was no way I was going to let Tasha come between me and Adrian. I had come too far to turn back now. This bitch had to be stopped.

I just couldn't understand it; I thought she would be happy to see that her brother and her best friend had found true love regardless of the facts at hand. If she could just accept the fact that Adrian and I are happy we could be the sisters that we always called each other as kids, but noooo she wanna try and blow my damn cover. Bitches stay hatin', they can't stand to see a sista come up.

I had finally come to grips with the fact that I had completely lost it. I was actually sitting here contemplating on killing my best friend.

Over the next few days I would be hit with a brigade of emotions. I teetered between rage, depression, sadness, and fear which would prove to be the most powerful of them all.

I had finally gotten the man that I love to love me back and I wasn't about to give that up. I cringed at the very thought of doing bodily harm to Tasha but she just didn't understand. She was beautiful and getting boyfriends came with ease for her. She didn't understand what it was like to long for someone for so many years and not have them give you the time of day. She didn't know what it meant to have her heart aching and pining over her one true love only to have him dismiss her like she didn't exist.

Now that Adrian thought I was a woman he had come full circle. And I knew deep in my heart that I would never find another man that loved me the way he did, or I him. She left me no choice. It was settled. I would have to kill Tasha.

I don't know if I was being driven by love, rage, or pure insanity but for some reason I didn't have any fear for what I was about to do. I found so many reasons to justify murder for the sake of love.

I would spend the next few days deciding on how I was going to do it as well casing her house and watching her pattern. She left for work every morning at the same time. And she always came out to warm her car up ahead of time. It was still dark this time of morning so it would make it easy for me to go undetected. I had made up my mind; tomorrow I was sending Tasha to meet her maker.

My weapon of choice would be a butcher's knife that I spent an hour sharpening the night before. I owned a gun but I didn't want to risk drawing attention to myself from the noise. I only had a few more days before she was threatening to tell Adrian everything so there wasn't any time to hatch a plan to poison her. I needed to move quickly and put this bitch down before she fucked up my fairytale.

The plan was set. I would arrive at her house before she left in the morning while it was still dark. I needed to find myself a hiding spot plus survey the area for any witnesses. If there were any neighbors out the plan might have to be halted. She wouldn't be hard to take down if I surprised her seeing as she was only 5'1 and I was 5'8 and much stronger. Much to my advantage I still possessed the strength of a man. This would prove to be valuable in slicing her throat with one quick swipe.

The outfit I chose was all black everything. A black track suit, black shoes, black gloves and a black face mask. I had to make sure I wasn't recognized if push came to shove and someone saw me. I got up super early that day and after getting dressed I took off on foot with a duffle bag in hand. It was still pitch black outside so I blended in perfectly.

I had already surveyed the area to make sure there weren't any loud ass barking dogs that would give me away as well. Thank God there wasn't any snow outside so I didn't have to worry about leaving footprints.

The plan to make her death seem like a robbery went off without a hitch. I lurked in the shadows beside her side door. She never even suspected that I was there when she came out the first time to start her car. When she came out the second time to leave I pounced.

In one fast swoop I covered her mouth and slit her throat at the same time. The jagged edge of the blade seared though her flesh like melted butter. Her blood was warm as it spilled to the ground and onto my exposed wrists. I loved my friend so I wanted to make it as quick and painless as possible. There was no need to prolong her suffering. When I hit the jugular the blood spurted like a water fountain. Once she fell to the ground it became surreal for me. Tasha was dead.

I quickly emptied the contents of her purse and snatched up her wallet. My heart raced and my palms were sweating profusely inside the leather gloves. My eyes darted around the immediate area to make sure the coast was clear before fleeing the scene.

Crazy In Love

"Although we've come to the end of the road…….Tasha I can't let you go….it's unnatural, you belong to me, and I belong to yoooouuuu."

These were the lyrics I sang as I burned the clothes I had worn along with Tasha's wallet. Once I scrubbed the scent of death and smoke from off of my body this would all be a distant memory. Adrian and I could get on with our life without any interruptions. My only regret was the fact that I had to witness how tore up my baby was over his sister's death. He vowed to catch the person who had done this to her. I knew this would never happen seeing as how I had covered my tracks. And with me here to comfort him, I knew my boo was gonna be alright.

Present day

Lao Tzo said that new beginnings are often disguised as painful endings. Although Tasha's death had a tremendous impact on her family, especially her brother, there was no denying the fact that Adrian and I had not only found love but he had taken it a step further and married a woman who made him happy in every way, a woman who would complete him. That woman was me. These basic bitches out here didn't have shit on me. I had to make some hard choices for love but in the end it was well worth it.

What's that you say? If given the chance would I do it all again? In a heartbeat. Don't hate the player, hate the game. Don't get mad at a bitch like me 'cause she did what she had to do, not only to get her man; but to keep him as well. It was gonna be smooth sailing from here on out.

"I love you Mrs. Pebbles Michelle Ramsey" Adrian proclaimed as he held up his glass of champagne to toast our union as man and wife.

"I love you too Mr. Adrian Ramsey."

After we toasted we shared a tender kiss before he made a statement that would leave me frozen in my tracks.

"I'm ready for little AJ."

"AJ?"

"Yep, Adrian Junior. I'm ready for you to start having my babies woman."

"*What the fuck?*" I thought to myself. The whole time I had worked this scheme I never once factored in that he might want kids. Why wouldn't he? I was so worried about deceiving him into thinking I was the perfect woman…. a real woman that I was in my own little world. It never crossed my mind that he would someday want a family of his own. What the hell was I going to do now?

The End

Midnite Love

Made in the USA
Lexington, KY
17 July 2016

Part Three: Jab-Step/1 Dribble Pull-up

1. Player 1 starts on the right wing against defender (X1).
2. Player 1 attacks the defender up foot with a hard right foot jab-step.
3. Player 1 then explodes and takes one hard dribble right for a pull-up jump shot. (The one dribble can be done either to the left or right. Do the drill on both sides of the floor and with both feet.)

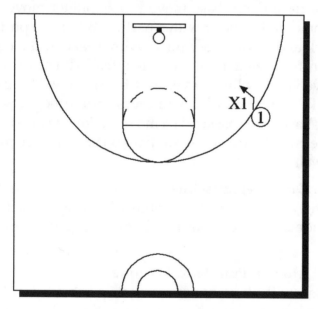

Post Series
From the Five-Star Basketball Archives

Purpose: These drill are designed to build offensive moves in the post, but skills can also be used away from the basket as well. Both post players and guards will benefit from this series.

Organization: Every base move has a counter move, which can be practiced alone or with a partner. Be sure to post above the block and begin every move with a fake in the opposite direction from which the move is intended. For example, if the move is a baseline move, start the move with a ball and head fake to the middle. All moves should begin with the player's back to the basket. The moves following are described from the right block, adjust so that you can practice from the left as well.

Move 1: Drop Step, Baseline
Long wide step on the baseline toward the basket, with a two-handed power dribble. Finish the move with a power lay-up.

Counter Move 1: Pull-Back, Baseline
Begin with the same movements as above, but lean toward the basket fake as if you were going to dribble the ball, but do not dribble. After faking the dribble, swing your lead foot (the foot you stepped with) toward the middle to square your shoulders and take a nice fade-away jumper. This can be a bank shot or over the rim.

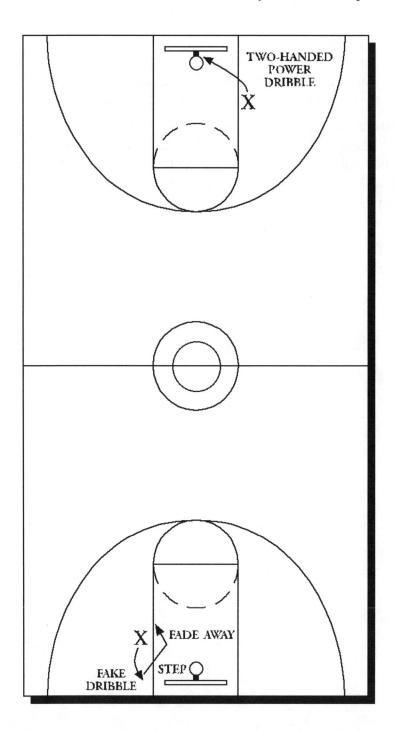

Move 2: Drop Step, Middle

Low wide step toward the middle of the floor. Extend and cover ground (seal the defense). Square your shoulders and make a power lay-up over the front of the rim.

Counter Move 2: Pull-Back, Middle

Begin with the same movements above, then lunge with a fake dribble to the middle of the lane. Swing your lead foot toward the baseline, square shoulders and take a fade-away jumper.